The RATS

of Meadowsweet Farm

The RATS
of Meadowsweet Farm

Dick King-Smith

Illustrations by Victor Ambrus

Barrington Stoke

First published in 2015 in Great Britain by
Barrington Stoke Ltd
18 Walker Street, Edinburgh, EH3 7LP

www.barringtonstoke.co.uk

This story was first published in a different form in
Muck and Magic (Heinemann, 1995)

Text © 1995 Fox Busters Ltd
Illustrations © 2015 Victor Ambrus

The moral right of Dick King-Smith and Victor Ambrus to
be identified as the author and illustrator of this work has
been asserted in accordance with the Copyright, Designs and
Patents Act, 1988

A CIP catalogue record for this book is available
from the British Library upon request

ISBN: 978-1-78112-417-8

Printed in China by Leo

This book has dyslexia friendly features

Contents

Chapter 1
Muck

Farmer Green had grey hair and a red face. The clothes he wore were always brown. This was in part because they had started out brown, and in part because they were covered in cow muck and pig muck. Now and again they were spotted with white, which was chicken muck.

Farmer Green only ever had a bath when there was an "H" in the month. But, to be fair, he often took several baths in March to make up for the rest of the year.

It was lucky that Mrs Green had been kicked on the nose by a cow when she was young, so she had no sense of smell.

Farmer Green's dogs thought his smell was lovely – a mix of sweaty body and filthy clothes and the beautiful rich smell of the dung-heap.

The dung-heap was at the very heart of Meadowsweet Farm. It stood in the middle of the farmyard, it looked like a huge plum cake and, my word, was it fruity!

Farmer Green put all the dung from the cow shed and the pig sty and the chicken house onto the dung-heap, and every other sort of stuff that would rot down and turn into lovely rich manure.

He flung addled eggs upon it, and dead chicks too, and rotten apples, and all kinds of household waste like tea leaves and bacon rinds and fish skins and potato peelings and, in hot weather, milk gone sour and stock gone bad.

And when Mrs Green killed a chicken or Farmer Green shot a rabbit, onto the dung-heap went feathers and skins and guts.

Dark brown liquid oozed from the base of the heap, and little wisps of steam rose from its top as the great cake cooked.

Chapter 2
Heaven

There were certain animals on the farm that thought the dung-heap was Heaven.

These were the rats. Meadowsweet Farm was running with rats.

As well as being dirty, Farmer Green was a wasteful, careless man, who would always rather not bother than take trouble. He did not store corn or pig-meal or cow-cake in metal bins, but left them in sacks. These sacks were no protection against sharp teeth. So the rats always had masses of food to eat, as well as all the lovely rotten titbits they found on the dung-heap.

The rats of Meadowsweet Farm were of all sizes, from babies to big old bucks. But whatever their ages, all the rats had one thing in common. They were fat.

They were also much too clever for Farmer Green. He put down poison for them, but they never touched it. He set traps for them, but they never sprung them.

Things might have been different
if there had been cats around, as there
are on almost every farm. But Farmer
Green didn't like cats.

"Can't stand 'em," he would say.
"Too clean by half. Forever washing
themselves, they are. Tisn't natural."

Chapter 3
Ripper

And so, over the many years that Farmer Green was at Meadowsweet Farm, the rats multiplied and grew fatter, bigger and stronger. The big bucks and does had bigger and bigger children, who in turn grew up to have bigger children yet.

But one rat was by far the biggest of all.

It sometimes happens when a great many rats are gathered together that one day a monster appears. He is always a male, and so huge that he dwarfs all others.

He is rat-like in every way, except that he is the size of a small dog. He rules the colony, takes his pick of the does as mates, and indeed deals out death to any rat that offends him.

This monster is known as the
king rat. There was such a one at
Meadowsweet Farm, and his name was
Ripper.

Farmer Green had never set eyes on the king rat. Ripper was far too cunning. He knew what the farmer's gun did to rabbits, and he had no wish to finish up on the dung-heap. So he kept to his den by day, and he only came out after dark.

Ripper was much too big to get down an ordinary rat-hole, but he had found a perfect hiding place. The chicken house backed onto a wall, and between house and wall there was a narrow space filled with weeds. Among these weeds a fox had dug a hole that tunnelled right under the chicken house.

'One night,' that fox must have thought, 'Mrs Green might forget to shut up her chickens, and then I will be nice and handy.'

What that fox had not expected was to return from hunting early one morning to find his tunnel had been taken over.

From the entrance came a strong smell of rat. The fox raced down the tunnel, eager to kill the intruder and breakfast off rat meat. But he got the shock of his life.

The fox was met by a monstrous creature almost as big as himself. It showed all its very large teeth and chattered at him in fury. The fox fled.

Chapter 4
The Army

By day, Ripper kept to his den, where he rat-napped in between visits from his troops. The king rat had organised the rats of Meadowsweet Farm into a private army. The most intelligent among the younger animals made up his personal bodyguard.

Not that Ripper's great body needed guarding – he was quite capable of looking after himself. But these young rats all had special duties.

Some acted as look-outs, keeping watch on Farmer Green and his wife and the dogs all day long.

Some acted as reporters, bringing news of everything that happened on the farm – a lorry delivering corn or meal, the latest traps or poison bait, new titbits on the dung-heap.

And some were the king rat's servants, bringing tasty morsels of food for him, which they carried in their mouths.

One morning, a young buck made its way down into the tunnel and squeaked for permission to enter the royal den.

"Come in!" Ripper growled. "What is it?"

"Please, sir," the young buck said, "there's a dead hen in the chicken house above."

"Fell off its perch, eh?" said Ripper. "I thought I heard a bump in the night. Right then, wait till they throw the bird on the dung-heap, then see that the heart and liver are brought to me, understand?" He licked his lips.

"Yes, sir," the young buck said. It was about to turn to go when it remembered the correct way to leave the royal chamber, and it backed out of the den.

Chapter 5
The Dead Hen

When Mrs Green came to let out the flock, she saw the dead hen on the floor of the chicken house and picked it up by its cold yellow legs. She carried it down to the yard and flung it on the dung-heap.

Farmer Green caught sight of her doing this as he finished milking the cows with his filthy dirty hands, and an idea struck him.

He went into the farmhouse and fetched his gun. Then he entered the stable and climbed the steps to the loft above. The window of this loft gave a perfect view of the yard below and the dung-heap in its centre and the dead hen in the middle of the dung-heap.

Farmer Green loaded both barrels,
sat down on an old box and waited.

For a while nothing happened.

The morning sun rose higher in the sky, and the only sounds to be heard were cluckings or gruntings now and then, or the low of a cow. Sparrows chirped on the stable roof. The smell of the dung-heap filled the air.

Then all of a sudden, rats began
to emerge from buildings all around
the yard. Some knew of the king rat's
orders. Some had only heard that there
was a dead hen to be had. Some knew
nothing but were simply following their
fellows.

Up onto the dung-heap climbed a host of brown shapes with scaly tails. Their heads raised as they sniffed, whiskers twitching. Then, with a rush, they flung themselves upon the carcass of the hen.

There was a chorus of squeaks and squeals as, in a cloud of feathers, they tore at the body. Those who had heard

the king's orders cried out – "Not the heart or the liver! Keep the heart and the liver for the king!"

Farmer Green waited until the excitement was at its peak, until a scrum of rats was fighting over the hen in a solid mass. Then he poked out his gun from the window of the loft and fired both barrels into the mob.

Chapter 6
Breakfast

Ripper was in his den, waiting for his breakfast to be served, when he heard the crash of the gun. Then, after a while, there was a nervous squeak in the tunnel. When Ripper roared that the rat could enter, he saw that it was not the original messenger, but a scared young doe.

"Well?" Ripper said. "What was the man shooting at? Rabbits?"

"No, sir," the doe said.

"What then?" Ripper said. "And where's my breakfast? The heart and liver from that hen, that's what I ordered. Where are they? Where's that young fellow I gave the orders to? I suppose he's gone and let the rest of them eat the lot? I'll kill him, see if I don't!"

"Please, sir," the young doe said, "he's already dead. Along with a great crowd

of them. On the dung-heap. The man shot them all. There are 30 dead rats there, sir. Please, sorry, sir."

For a while there was an awful silence in the fox tunnel. Ripper crouched in the gloom, and it seemed to the young doe that he was staring right through her. In fact, Ripper was not seeing her at all. He did not notice as she backed away.

All Ripper saw, in his mind's eye, was a ghastly pile of bodies on top of the dung-heap. 30 bodies, no less. 30 of his bravest and best rats.

"He will pay!" Ripper snarled. "That man, he will pay for this!"

Chapter 7
Revenge

By night, the numbers of rats had fallen by more than 30. Another dozen had left the farm to find some other place to live. These were the look-outs who had failed in their duties. They should have seen the farmer go in and fetch his gun, then reported it to the king. But they hadn't, and they knew the penalty for such a failure was death.

At dusk, Ripper came out of his den in a fury. He sent messengers with orders that every rat was to come to the barn at moonrise.

In silence they waited, rank upon rank of them, every eye upon the king rat. He crouched above them on a pile of straw bales, unmoving, menacing.

At last he spoke.

"Rats of Meadowsweet Farm," said
Ripper. His voice was so harsh that the
hungry white owl who was perched on
the roof timbers, looking down at them
all, flew hastily out of the barn.

"Tonight we are gathered together," the king went on, "to mourn the loss of 30 brave comrades. Those who caused their deaths would also be dead by now had they not fled like the cowards they are."

Here Ripper paused and looked at each rat in turn, and each rat in turn felt a cold thrill of fear.

Then the king rat spoke again.

"If there are cowards left among you," he said softly, "come forward."

No one moved.

"Good," Ripper said. "For you will need all your courage. Tonight we seek revenge upon the man who murdered your mates. Listen carefully, each and every one of you."

Chapter 8
A Daring Plan

Ripper's plan was a daring one – he planned to invade the farmhouse itself. He aimed to do maximum damage, first to the house, and then to the farmer himself.

Because Farmer Green was so lazy and slipshod, the house at Meadowsweet Farm was practically falling down.

There were holes and gaps and broken panes everywhere, where rats could enter with ease.

Ripper's orders to his troops were to get inside the house – the dogs were chained to their kennels in the yard – and do the greatest possible damage.

"Eat any food you can find," he said, "and if you cannot eat it, foul it. Foul the carpets also, and chew holes in the furnishings, and spoil and destroy wherever you go. And if you find electric wires, bite through them."

'Biting the wires will kill you, I'm afraid,' Ripper thought. But, like any General, he knew that soldiers must die in battle.

Then he called for volunteers.

"I want good climbers," he said, and a chorus of voices cried, "Me, sir! Me, sir! Me!"

Ripper picked ten rats from these.

"Your job," he said, "will be to scale the wall of the house – there is creeper on it, to make things easier. Climb in the open window of the room where the man and woman sleep."

"Shall we attack them, sir?" one eager rat asked.

"No," Ripper said. "Hide under the bed, all of you, and keep still and quiet. Then, in the early morning, when the man gets out of bed to go and milk his cows, wait till he is at the top of the stairs. Then rush at him, squeak and squeal and bite at his ankles, and with any luck he will fall down the stairs."

"And if, as I suspect," Ripper went on, "they are steep, and because he is heavy and clumsy, he will, I hope, break his neck."

Chapter 9
Alarm

Ripper waited until the small hours before he sent in the first of his troops. They had orders to avoid the dogs, and to do their work as silently as possible. They did it well.

Just before dawn, Ripper sent up the climbing patrol. By the time Farmer Green's old tin alarm clock went off at 5 a.m., ten rats were under the bed, waiting.

It was still dark, so the farmer pressed the light switch, but nothing happened. Downstairs lay the burned body of the rat who had bitten through the mains supply.

"Electric's off," Farmer Green said to his wife. "And there's a terrible smell of rat in here."

"I can't smell anything," Mrs Green said sleepily.

Farmer Green got dressed – he needed only to pull on his trousers, for he always slept in shirt, socks and pants. Then he went out of the bedroom in his stockinged feet.

Ten rats followed silently. As Farmer Green reached the top of the stairs, feeling his way in the darkness, the rats charged.

Mrs Green heard a chorus of squeals and a loud curse from her husband, and then the thumping, bumping noise of a heavy body tumbling down the stairs.

Then there was silence.

Chapter 10
A Nice Bath

Mrs Green never forgot that dreadful day.

First, she found her husband upon the floor at the foot of the stairs. Then she dialled 999 and waited for the ambulance.

And then she discovered all the damage done in the kitchen and the other downstairs rooms of the farmhouse.

There were holes in the chair covers and in the curtains. Little ornaments lay smashed on the floor. Books had been tipped from their shelves and their pages had been shredded, and there was rat muck everywhere.

As for the food in the larder, cheeses had been nibbled, eggs broken and sucked dry, and what was left of a big pan of cream was speckled with rat droppings.

Once the ambulance had left, Mrs Green went to milk the cows. When this was done, she set herself to tidy up.

At the hospital, they held their noses and worked out that Farmer Green was suffering from concussion but had no bones broken. Then they first of all sprayed him with Spring Violets air freshener.

Then, once he had come round, they stripped off all his clothes and burned them.

And then they saw to it that he gave himself a very good wash all over in a bath – even though it was only July. They had to change the water several times.

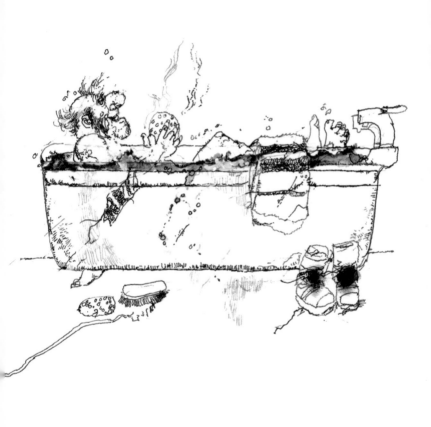

Later that day, they sent Farmer Green home to Meadowsweet Farm. He was dressed in clean hospital pyjamas and he smelled like a big, pink, newly washed baby. (Mrs Green could not know this, of course.)

Husband and wife sat at the kitchen table, drinking tea.

Mrs Green looked at her husband's face, at his neck, his hands, his fingernails. "You look different," she said.

Farmer Green ran his fingers over his clean hair, and felt the bump where his head had struck the floor. His injury, it seemed, had changed him for the better.

"I feels different," he said. "Reckon I'll have a bath a bit more often. Tis nice."

"It was rats," said Mrs Green.

"Was it?" her husband said. He seemed to have forgotten the whole thing.

"You'll have to shoot some more," Mrs Green said. "They made a mess."

"Not now," said Farmer Green. "I do feel a bit tired."

"Well, go to bed then," said Mrs Green.

"All right. But you go up first, and mind and put nice clean sheets and blankets on the bed. I don't want to get meself dirty."

Chapter 11
Both Triggers

When her husband was in bed, Mrs Green went out to shut up her chickens as the light faded. All of a sudden she saw a large brown shape come out from behind the chicken house and glide away along the bottom of the wall. Ripper was on his way to congratulate his troops.

Mrs Green shut up the chickens and returned to the farmhouse. She fetched her husband's gun, loaded it and came quietly back.

"It looked like a rat," she said to herself, "but no rat was ever so big as that. Maybe twas a badger. Anyways, I'll bet he was after my hens."

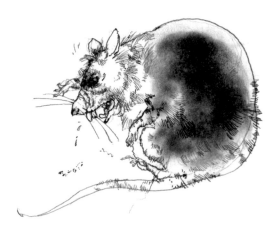

And she waited.

In a little while the moon rose, and not long after Mrs Green saw the large brown shape slink back along beneath the wall. She waited until the creature was within point-blank range, and then she pressed both triggers.

The recoil from the gun was so great that she fell over backwards.

As for Ripper, the king rat, he fell dead.

Somehow Mrs Green managed to heave his body up on top of the dung-heap, where it lay among the bodies of

the rats her husband had shot, its great teeth bared in a grin of death.

It was a weary Mrs Green who dragged herself up to bed that night. Her shoulder was bruised by the gun and her back and arms were sore from the effort of lugging the body of her victim to the dung-heap.

She climbed into bed beside her husband, who smelled so sweet, but she was unaware of it. "I shot ever such a big rat," she said.

"Oh ah?" said Farmer Green sleepily.

"We'll have to get rid of them, you know," said Mrs Green.

"Of what?"

"Rats."

"Oh ah."

But the strange thing is that the Greens had no need to do anything about the rats.

It must have been the sight of the dead body of their king, because when the sun rose on the following morning, there was not a single one left – and nor did one ever return – out of all the rats of Meadowsweet Farm.